Coyote Boy

An Original Trickster Story

Coyote Boy

An Original Trickster Story

Written & Illustrated by
Deron *Sasonake* Douglas

Coyote Boy: An Original Trickster Story

Written & Illustrated by Deron Sasonake Douglas - Copyright © 2015
Edited by Mae Argilan

ISBN-13: 978-1-77115-218-1

1. First Nations - Aboriginal - Juvenile fiction - fantasy

A First Edition
January 28th, 2015

Published by
Bear Spirit Press
PO Box 54016
1-5762 Highway 7 East
Markham, Ontario L3P 7Y4 Canada
http://www.BearSpiritPress.com

Bear Spirit Press was created with the intention of giving voice to the many Aboriginal authors, illustrators, artists and storytellers on Turtle Island, and has a special interest in publishing quality Aboriginal literature that expresses the highest degree of cultural authenticity and truthfulness. Bear Spirit Press is proudly Kanien'kehá:ka owned and operated.

Shé:kon:

Before we begin, it is important to understand that not all First Nations are the same either culturally or economically. Therefore, some aspects presented within this book should be taken as applicable only to the Mohawk culture, with the exception of Coyote. The author could find no comparative Coyote equivalent within the Mohawk or Iroquois cultures, so has taken artistic license by including Coyote within the story. He has however tried to remain *authentic* within the context of the Coyote figure as presented by other First Nation stories.

Within these cultures Coyote is generally a teacher of hidden wisdom who uses humour and trickery to teach those around him a valuable life lesson. While Coyote is a major figure for most First Nations, his characteristics do vary greatly from culture to culture. In some cultures Coyote is revered as a hero who creates, teaches and helps humans, while in others he is an anti-hero who demonstrates the dangers of certain negative behaviours such as greed, recklessness and arrogance. Other cultures may portray him as a trickster whose lack of wisdom often gets him in trouble, and whose 'tricks' tend to backfire.

In the end the author feels that Coyote is a lovable character and one that the boy can learn many important lessons from.

Please note that the author does not consider himself a spokesperson for either the Mohawk Nation or all things Native, but is presenting his views and stories as he has heard them. - Sasonake

This is for my Dad.

Nia:wen'kó:wa, Konnorónhkwa

Acknowledgements

I would like to thank Keith Secola for allowing me to use the lyrics from his song *NDN Kars*.

Although I remember my father listening to songs such as *King of the Road* and *Moon River* while we travelled, I felt that *NDN Kars* would be more appropriate to the spirit of the story.

Please visit Keith's site at http://www.secola.com and give his music a try for a taste of *Contemporary Native American* music. *Chi-miigwech.*

I would also like to thank my friend Mae Argilan for her help in editing this story and for her excitement when asked. *Thank you.*

Finally, I would like to thank Taiaiake Alfred for his encouragement and suggestions. *Niawen'kó:wa Cuz.*

There once was a boy who lived in a far away land, a land that was not his original home. This isn't to say that he lived on another planet, or in the trees, or in the sea.

He lived in a rather ordinary house, on top of an ordinary hill, that was covered in ordinary grass, in a small ordinary town that was not yet a town.

Through the boy's eyes this house was not so ordinary, it did not sit on top of an ordinary hill, nor was it covered in ordinary grass, and the small town was not so ordinary, even though it was not yet a town.

To this boy his new home was mysterious and exciting.

The house was a rich dusty rose, and it sat atop a high majestic hill surrounded by long flowing grass that waved in the evening breeze like the hairs of his dog *Okwa:ri*.

At night the sky shone with a million billion stars that sparkled like diamonds of sunlight cast upon the waters of the St. Lawrence River in summer. And if he was lucky and paid close attention to the sky, he would see a shooting star streak across with a blazing tail of multi-colored sparks.

Best of all, when the sun went to bed and the moon came out to play, the boy could look out into the yard and see quick bursts of amber sparks flick through the evening grass.

The fireflies were the most magical of all the Creator's creatures, and the boy loved nothing more than to watch as they floated on the cooling currents of twilight.

This new home on the hill was a magical place. Though the boy still missed his old home with his friends and family, his babysitter and his aunt that lived just next door.

This was a Mohawk boy, and his original home was on the *Rez*, as he often heard it called. In this place he felt safe and secure as though everyone were his family.

On the *Rez* he could safely ride his mini-bike from one end to the other and no one would mind; not even the police who were called 'Peace Keepers'. They would often wave and smile to him as he drove by searching for adventure.

If he was far from home someone would ask if he was hungry or thirsty, and if so, they would give him a snack. The best thing about the *Rez* was that he could explore his world without worry, because everyone knew everyone else, and they always looked out for each other.

In the evening, when the sun was just setting and the air began to cool, his father would take him down to the lacrosse fields to watch the teenagers as they ran up and down the fields with lacrosse sticks in hand chasing a ball in mock battle. Sometimes they would use a special ball that they would set on fire and he could watch in amazement as they tossed it around in the deepening dark.

But best of all, if he was really good his father would take him to the ice cream store for a single scoop or two. Dressed only in his *PJs* he would sit in the back of the old beaten up Beetle and watch as the long grass sped past his open window. From this place he could smell the cool air of the approaching night, and listen to the honk of his father's horn as they passed through the tunnel under the highway signalling their exit from *Kahnawà:ke.*

24

One day his mother and father decided, for reasons beyond the understanding of the boy, that it was time to leave their home on the *Rez*.

So, packing up all the family's things in their beaten up old Beetle, the father took his wife and the boy and travelled from their home on the *Rez* to the small ordinary town, that was not yet a town.

And so…

...they passed through the tunnel as the boy had many times before, and the father gave the horn one last honk as they left *Kahnawà:ke* for the last time.

The boy loved to travel, and so he curled up on the back seat of the Beetle. There he listened to his parents talk of their future and listen to the radio as his father sang along.

Sometimes the father would tell the boy stories about how he would leave their home on the *Rez* and travel through the night to New York City so that he could find a job as an iron worker.

The boy loved these stories, and imagined how his father and his uncles would walk along the skeletal beams of the unfinished buildings more than 100 floors above the ground. So high the boy imagined, that even Eagle dared not follow.

He especially liked the story of how his father would hang from a ledge only a few inches wide, while holding a red hot rivet so that his uncle could hammer it in place with a jack hammer.

The boy was familiar with the summer rhythm on the *Rez*. It was a time when his father would stay all week in New York City, then return home late Friday night only to leave once again after Sunday dinner.

On this trip, however, the boy only listened to the radio, the hum of the engine, and the vibration of the wheels as they beat out a tempo like the heartbeat of the Pow Wow.

And soon he fell asleep...

NDN POWER
I'VE BEEN DRIVING IN MY INDIAN CAR
THE POUND OF THE WHEEL DRUMMING IN MY BRAIN
MY DASH IS DUSTY, MY PLATES ARE EXPIRED
PLEASE MR. OFFICER, LET ME EXPLAIN
I GOT TO MAKE IT TO THIS POW WOW TONIGHT
I'LL BE SINGING 49, DOWN BY THE RIVERSIDE
LOOKING FOR A SUGAR, RIDING IN MY INDIAN CAR ...
GOT MY T-BIRD ON THE DASHBOARD, I AIN'T GOT NO SPARE
GOT A FEATHER FROM AN EAGLE, I AIN'T GOT NO CARE
THE ROAD IS EMPTY IN MY BOTTLE OF DESIRE
DAYLIGHT IS BREAKING, THE SUN TOUCHES FIRE
I GOT TO MAKE ANOTHER POW WOW TONIGHT
I'LL BE SINGING 49, DOWN BY THE RIVERSIDE ...

The next morning the boy awoke curled up on the back seat of the car with sunshine in his eyes. To his surprise the car had stopped moving!

Rubbing the sleep from his eyes, the boy lifted his head and looked out the window. He discovered that they were parked in front of a small house that looked newer than anything he had ever seen before.

Ahead of him at the foot of the long stone driveway his father and mother were talking to a man in a business suit. Quietly getting out of the car he stretched his back, wiggled his toes, yawned a morning yawn and sat on the front step waiting for them to return.

He watched intently as he tried to figure out what they were doing. Just as he was about to get up and ask, his father and mother shook hands with the man and walked towards the house. His father beckoned excitedly and rushed to the door of their new home.

The boy had never seen his parents so happy, and to his surprise the father scooped up his mother and carried her through the open doorway as they all laughed and giggled.

As time passed, the routine of daily life settled in as it normally does. The boy's father no longer worked on the tall buildings in New York City, but instead found a job in an office building during the day, while attending night school in the evenings.

At night, when the father came home from work, and after they had eaten their dinner, the father and the mother and the boy would sit outside on the front step of their new home. His parents would sit and drink a pot of tea and talk about their day, while the boy listened intently and the crickets chirped in the background.

This was the boy's favourite part of the day. He would sit on the bottom step, still within hearing distance of his parent's conversation, but close enough to the grass so he could get a good view of the fireflies as they flitted around and danced their evening dance.

If he was lucky, a firefly would get really close and he could carefully cup it in his hand and watch as the light from its tiny tail blinked on and off like bursting soap bubbles in the sky.

One of those nights, when the crickets were chirping and a gentle breeze blew through the sweet-smelling grass, the boy found himself sitting alone on the lower step watching the fireflies.

He wondered what kind of animals could be hiding in the tall grass. Just as this thought cleared his mind, he heard the gentle rustle of leaves and the parting of the sweet grass.

Peering into the darkness, the boy saw two glowing yellow eyes. Sitting on his haunches, and staring at the boy, sat a coyote.

"*Shé:kon*. This is the first time I've seen you here," says Coyote.

"Yes, this is our new home. My father brought us here so that he could work inside an office building instead of on the outside of one. How can you speak?" the boy asks.

"That was very wise of your father, the view is generally good, but that's about it," says the coyote, with a chuckle. "I am Coyote, and I have always spoken? But these days very few people care to listen. They've forgotten the old stories, and only know what Hollywood has told them. Most of that stuff is twisted, so the truth is no longer known. I bet the only coyote you know is the one with the bird that goes beep-beep?"

The boy ponders this for a minute. Scratches his head, and then ponders it some more.

"I guess you're right," the boy said. "My *tóta* used to know many stories, and she told them to me all the time. But she's gone now, and there is no one left to do this."

"That is indeed sad. Though she must have taught you well. Most young people would rather watch TV or play with the Internet," says Coyote. "You are a rare person indeed, since you have chosen to listen."

And so Coyote and the boy became friends. They talked for many hours that night about the world and how Turtle Island had changed, and how the people stopped listening to the animals and how the animals felt that the people had lost their connection to the heartbeat of Mother Earth.

When the boy's parents came outside a few minutes later they found their son fast asleep on the lower step. Fireflies were dancing around his head and only the rustling of the leaves, and the parting of the sweet grass could be heard.

For the rest of the summer the boy did not see Coyote.

Soon the leaves fell, the days grew colder, and winter covered the yard with a blanket of snow.

The boy could no longer sit on his lower step and watch the fireflies dance in the moonlight. Instead, he sat in his favourite window and watched the snowflakes cover the ground, and wondered what had happened to his new friend Coyote.

One evening, after his mother and father had fallen fast asleep, the boy awoke to the sound of the wind rustling through the grass. Wondering what it could be, he slipped out of bed, went to the front hall, and quietly stepped out the front door and onto the porch to investigate.

Even though it was still winter, the boy did not feel the cold as it wrapped around him like a blanket. Instead he thought, *What a beautiful night.*

Running out to the front lawn he jumped up, spread his arms, and exclaimed, "Hello Brave Hunters! Hello Great Bear! I see that you are still being chased. Run now, run clever bear before you are caught. And remember me!"

Behind him a full moon was rising. It shone brightly and reflected off the snow creating crystalline droplets of glistening star dust along a thin layer of frozen crust. Turning around the boy saw the faint glow of familiar yellow eyes approaching from across the yard.

"Coyote, I am so happy to see you ," the boy said, in a booming voice.

"*Kwe Kwe*. I'm glad that you remember me. I thought that perhaps the Internet had entranced you and you were tangled up in your video game cords unable to move, while calling out my name. Coyote...Coyote... why have you forgotten me?" says Coyote, with a grin.

"No, Coyote, I haven't forgotten you. Would you like a doggie biscuit?" the boy says, with a smirk.

Annoyed Coyote replies, "Only if I can taste a finger or two along with that doggie biscuit. Come with me now, and I'll show you something you might like."

The boy followed Coyote. They travelled across the snow and through the fields, flying across its surface with barely a step. The boy found that he could easily keep up with Coyote without exerting himself.

Startled by his own speed, the boy looked down at his feet and saw that they were not leaving imprints in the deep snow. To his amazement he realized that they were both skimming across the fields like the shadow of a crow. Only their moonlit silhouettes dared to touch the frozen crust below.

"I am flying as fast as the wind," the boy exclaims. "How is this possible?"

As Coyote turned his head to respond, the boy saw the glow of yellow eyes and the glint of a mischievous smile. "We are travelling the way of the *old ones*, boy. Let's just call it, *Air Coyote*," he chuckles.

The boy did not yet know his friend's true nature, and his fondness for playing tricks on unsuspecting animals and humans alike.

They travelled over the snow for what seemed like many hours; boy following Coyote, a procession of quicksilver skimming across the surface with the sound of moonlight on cold crisp snow. Just as the boy was about to give up, Coyote stopped.

There before them was a frozen river that coiled through a forest with untouched banks of snow. As the boy approached Coyote, he jumped onto the frozen river and ran along it's course without fear of slipping.

Turning his head, Coyote taunts, "Follow me, boy. We are almost there!"

Together they ran along the river, the boy chasing Coyote as the *Three Brave Hunters* chased the *Great Bear*. With blurring swiftness the banks of snow soon turned to a lattice of wood like the outstretched arms of a bridal party.

Soon both boy and Coyote stopped. Ahead was a thick wall of fog, an unusual sight on a clear winter's night. Thinking nothing of it Coyote and the boy raced into the thick fog bank without hesitation.

Whiteness engulfed the boy, but it soon parted like his bedroom curtains in the morning.

The boy found himself in what appeared to be the same forest, along the same river, but now it was no longer winter. As he looked around in wonder he saw that the snow had magically melted and new leaves had sprouted in the blink of an eye. *Where am I?* the boy thought.

Looking ahead the boy spied Coyote waiting for him on a rock. To the boy's surprise, Coyote seemed a little different. His eyes shone a deeper yellow and he appeared to be carrying himself more like a very old man, rather than a scruffy old coyote.

Looking beyond Coyote, the boy spied a tree perched on an outcropping of rock. Unlike the other trees in the forest, this one shone with a brilliant white light that seemed to dance like the boy's fireflies in summer.

The boy immediately felt certain that this was a special tree beyond his understanding.

"Boy, allow me to give you something special. Take this tree and bring it home. Give it to your father and mother; they can use it as a Christmas tree. This is my gift to you as a friend," says Coyote.

"How can I do this, Coyote?" the boy asks. "This tree it is too tall for me to carry."

As those words left the boy's mouth, the swirling white light changed to a bright fiery orange and engulfed the tall tree to its very tip. The tree shuddered and shook, and before the boy's eyes, the tall tree shrunk to no more than three feet in height.

"What were you saying?" says Coyote. "Take the tree now. Even someone your size should be able to carry a three-foot tree?"

The boy carefully considered Coyote's words. The tree would look wonderful in their new home he thought, but the memory of one of his *tóta's* stories pulled at his mind.

"No, Coyote", the boy replied firmly. "I do not think this tree is yours to give. It is a great tree indeed, and even though you have made it small, I cannot take it for myself. There is something sacred about this tree that I cannot understand. Yet I know that it would be wrong for me to do this."

With those words the *Great Tree* grew to many times its previous size and burst through the dark into the sunlight above. It was so high that Eagle found its top and perched there to rest. Its branches stretched out to all corners of Turtle Island and its spirit sung out to the *Four Sky Dwellers* in a way that hadn't been heard in a very long time.

Seeing this, the boy knew that he had made the right choice, and that Coyote was only trying to trick him into doing something that would cause great mischief.

Feeling that it was time to leave, the boy turned to Coyote and said his goodbyes. "*Ó:nen* Coyote. Although you are a rascal, I think I'll see you again."

With that, the boy turned and ran back through the fog bank as he did before.

As the whiteness enveloped the boy, he felt his body float, and soon found himself lying on his soft comfortable bed with his favourite blanket tenderly pressing against his body. The boy thought about his new friend Coyote and knew that they would go on many new adventures together.

Next time he would be more careful, because he had learned that Coyote was a mischievous creature, who had almost tricked him into stealing *The Great Tree of the Sky-People.*

Before the boy closed his eyes, he thought he glimpsed for a very brief moment, the land of the *Sky-People* as they looked down on him and smiled an approving smile.

SUPPLEMENTAL INFORMATION

Coyote Boy is the story of a young Mohawk boy from *Kahnawà:ke* who moves away from the *Rez* to a small town in southern Ontario. *Kahnawà:ke* is located in Quebec on the south shore of the St. Lawrence River within 20 minutes driving distance of Montreal.

It is important to understand that not all First Nations are the same either culturally or economically. Therefore, some aspects presented within this book should be taken as applicable only to the Mohawk culture, with the exception of Coyote. The author could find no comparative Coyote equivalent within the Mohawk or Iroquois cultures, so has taken artistic license by including Coyote within the story. He has however tried to remain *authentic* within the context of the Coyote figure as presented by other First Nation stories.

Within these cultures Coyote is generally a teacher of hidden wisdom who uses humour and trickery to teach those around him a valuable life lesson. While Coyote is a major figure for most First Nations, his characteristics do vary greatly from culture to culture. In some cultures Coyote is revered as a hero who creates, teaches and helps humans, while in others he is an anti-hero who demonstrates the dangers of certain negative behaviours such as greed, recklessness and arrogance. Other cultures may portray him as a trickster whose lack of wisdom often gets him in trouble, and whose 'tricks' tend to backfire.

In the end the author feels that Coyote is a lovable character and one that the boy can learn many important lessons from.

The information presented within this supplement can be used for further discussion, or as reference material for further understanding of the story. The author has placed a small list of online resources at the back of the book if you are interested in learning more about the Iroquois Confederacy or the Mohawk First Nation specifically.

Please note that the author does not consider himself a spokesperson for either the Mohawk Nation or all things Native, but is presenting his views and stories as he has heard them.

MOHAWK WORDS USED WITHIN THE STORY

The Mohawk language is a member of the Iroquoian language group, which is made up of First Nation languages that are known to lack *labial consonants*. Labial consonants are consonants in which the lips are used to articulate a sound. It is important to note that while there are several First Nations within the Iroquoian language group, this does not imply that they are Iroquois or of the Iroquois Confederacy. This language classification is a product of colonialism and has caused some confusion in the past. For example, while the Huron people (Wyandot or Wendat) are a member of the Iroquoian language group, they are not members of the Iroquois Confederacy.

Iroquoian Language Family Groups

Southern Iroquoian
- Cherokee

Northern Iroquoian
  Lakes Iroquoian
    Five Nations
- Seneca
- Cayuga
- Onondaga
- Oneida
- Mohawk

Susquehannock
- Susquehannock

Huronian
- Wyandot (Huron–Petun)
- Wenrohronon
- Neutral
- Erie

Tuscarora–Nottoway
- Tuscarora
- Nottoway
- Laurentian

When reviewing the words below, it is important to remember that certain sounds represented by some English letters do not exist within the Mohawk language. For example: the "K" sound is pronounced "gah" or "ga", "ke" would be pronounced "gay" or "ge", and the "T" sound would be pronounced as a "D". The ":" indicates that the sound should be held longer.

So *Kahnawà:ke* would be pronounced "g ah-na-wa-gay", and *Kateri* is pronounced "gah-dah-ree" in *Kahnawà:ke* or "gah-dah-lee" in *Ahkwesàhsne*.

Okwa:ri [oh-kwa-re] – meaning 'bear'
Kahnawà:ke [gah-na-wa-gay] – 'place of the rapids'
Kahnawakero:non [gah-na-wa-gay-row-noon] – 'the people of *Kahnawake*'.

Shé:kon [seh-goh] – 'hello'
tóta [do-da] –'grandmother'
Kwe Kwe [gweh-gweh] – 'hi there'
Ó:nen [oh-na] – 'bye now' or 'bye'

THE IROQUOIS CONFEDERACY

The Iroquois Confederacy was originally composed of five First Nations (or "tribes" in the USA), the Mohawk, Oneida, Onondaga, Cayuga, and Seneca. In 1722 the Tuscarora Nation joined the Confederacy, thus affecting a change of name to 'The League of Six Nations'.

While the French call us 'The Iroquois Confederacy' and the English, 'The League of Six Nations', it should be noted that we called ourselves the 'Haudenosaunee', which means 'people of the long house'. The 'long house' is more than the structure that we lived in, but is a model for our social structure and spiritual beliefs. Additionally, while our languages are related within the Haudenosaunee, they do have slightly different dialects, and as a result a Mohawk would say "Lodeenosaunee" while a Seneca would say "Haudenosaunee".

The Iroquois flag is a representation of the geographic territorial boundaries of the Haudenosaunee Confederacy, indicating the order of each First Nation within the metaphorical 'longhouse'. As such, each Nation has a responsibility within the Haudenosaunee Confederacy. The Mohawks are the '*Keepers of the Eastern Door*', the Seneca are the '*Keepers of the Western Door*', and the Onondaga are the '*Keepers of the Central Fire*'. As the names imply, the Mohawk and Seneca acted as protectors from invading nations from either side, while the Onondaga maintain the government's capitol where the Chiefs and Elders still meet to discuss Haudenosaunee politics.

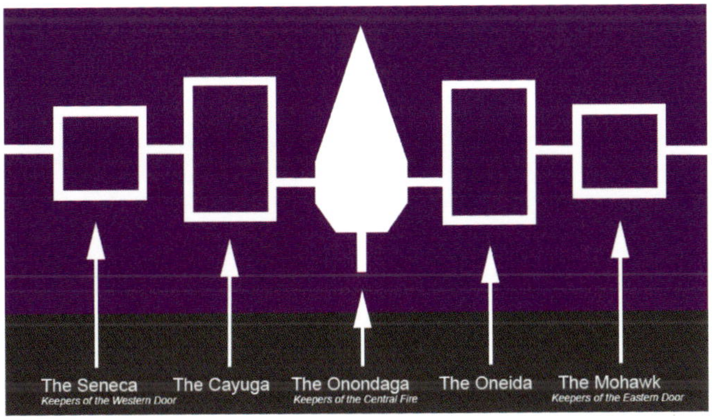

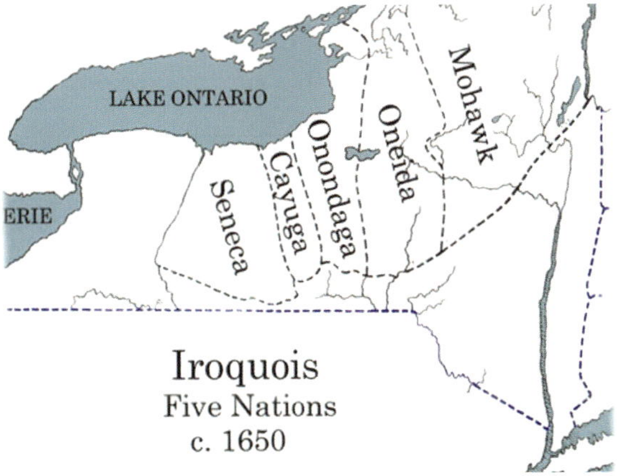

STORY REFERENCES

A number of Mohawk stories are referenced within *Coyote Boy*, and in order to give a fuller understanding to the reader, the author would like to present them here. These stories have been written in their oral form in order to duplicate the rhythm and expression of oral storytelling.

THE THREE BRAVE HUNTERS AND THE GREAT BEAR

(RETOLD BY SASONAKE)

Once, a long time ago, there was a small Mohawk village that sat by a river among the trees. One day one of the hunters went out looking for game and came across the footprints of a giant bear. This bear was larger than any he had ever seen before, and this caused him to worry. As he followed the tracks he noticed that they circled around the village, but he could not find where they originated.

Not long after, the village people soon noticed that the animals were disappearing from the forest, and that game was getting harder to find. Soon it would be winter and the villagers were worried that there would not be enough food to feed the people during the cold winter months. As fall approached, the meat racks were soon empty and there developed a scarcity of food in the village.

One of the Clan Mothers said, "We must send out our hunters to find this giant bear that is killing all the animals in the forest, or we will starve this winter. "

And so, a party of the bravest hunters were gathered and sent out in search of the giant bear. They travelled for many days, and eventually found the giant bear's den.

At once the air was filled with arrows as the hunters tried to kill the giant bear, but the arrows only bounced off the bear's hide, because it was so thick.

Now, as you can imagine, this really upset the bear, and he turned in rage and charged the hunters. All were killed, except for one hunter that escaped. He returned to the village and told the Clan Mothers of this *Great Bear*.

More hunters were sent out to kill the Great Bear, but they were also slain, unable to kill the him. This went on and on until there were few hunters left in the Mohawk village.

Soon all the deer vanished, and there was very little game left in the forest. As a result, the people in the village became very thin from lack of food, and starvation caused many to become sick and die.

One night, three brothers each had a strange dream in which they saw themselves track down and kill the Great Bear.

Because the Mohawk people believe in the truth of dreams, the three brothers said, "This dream is telling us what we must do. We must go out and hunt this Great Bear and kill him before everyone in the village dies from starvation."

And so, gathering their weapons and a small supply of food they set out to find the Great Bear.

Soon they came upon his tracks not far from the village and followed them with excitement. For many days they travelled until they came to the back end of Turtle Island.

Then one night, through a clearing in the woods, they saw the Great Bear climbing up a steep hill which lead to a cliff at the end of the world.

Running after the Great Bear, they shouted, "Run Great Bear, Run! You cannot escape your fate for we have dreamed of your death!"

Fearing for his life, the Great Bear ran and ran until he came to the edge of the cliff, which was the tail of Turtle Island, and seeing the three hunters approaching, he jumped high into the sky.

Seeing this, the three young brothers chased the Great Bear, and without hesitation, followed him into the sky.

From this time on you can still see those brothers and the bear.

When the Mohawk people see the Big Dipper in the sky, they say, "See, the *Three Brave Hunters* are still chasing the *Great Bear.*"

Note from the author: I enjoyed telling this story to my three sons, Jake, Jesse and Dylan when they were small. I would often tell them jokingly, that I would send them out to go bear racing if they misbehaved.

THE MOHAWK CREATION STORY

(RETOLD BY SASONAKE)

It should be noted that this creation story is particular to the people of the Haundenosaunee Confederacy, and that each First Nation outside of the Confederacy will have their own story. In addition, details of this particular story do change between the Mohawk, Oneida, Onondaga, Cayuga, and Seneca people, and in fact may change from storyteller to storyteller.

The following is how it was told to me by my father and I typically add my own details when I retell it. The overall structure of the story does however remain the same within each telling.

Once, a very long time ago, the world was very different from what it is today. In this world there were no people and no land. There was only water as far as the eye could see. And above this water floated a land we call *Sky-World*. In the middle of Sky-World grew a *Great Tree* with branches that stretched out from one end of Sky-World to the other, and each morning when the wind blew through its branches, one could hear singing as the wind passed through the pine needles of the tree.

Now, unlike the world of water below, Sky-World had people living on it that were very much like what would become humans today. They were called *Onkweshon*.

Two of these people were Sky-Woman and her husband. One day Sky-Woman became pregnant and like many pregnant women, she had cravings for certain foods.

Well, one day Sky-Woman went to her husband and said, "Husband, I am pregnant and I would very much like to taste the bark of the Great Tree. It is a special tree and I'm sure it must taste very good."

Although the husband cared for Sky-Woman he could not give her the bark of the Great Tree. For you see, while it had growing on it many different types of fruits and leaves, it was the husband's job to protect the tree and to stop anyone from eating from it. So, instead of giving into his wife's requests, he tried to satisfy her by bringing many different fruits and nuts from the other trees that were allowed.

But time and time again, Sky-Woman would not be satisfied with what her husband brought her, and she continued to insist that her husband bring her the bark of the Great Tree.

As you could imagine, the husband could take it no longer and he gave into his wife's wishes. Although he knew it was wrong he dug a big hole next to the Great Tree so that the roots could be uncovered, and a little bark could be scraped off to satisfy Sky-Woman.

He then called Sky-Woman. "Wife, come here! I cannot bear to damage the Great Tree because I have been given the job of protecting it. So, I've dug a hole and if you look into it you can see a small root with soft tasty bark. If you wish to taste this bark, you must reach in and get it for yourself."

Looking into the hole Sky-Woman saw that it went all the way through the bottom of Sky-World so that all she could see was water below. Wanting nothing more than to taste the succulent bark of the sacred tree, Sky-Woman reached down into the hole. Just as she was about to reach the root, her husband pushed her into the hole and out the bottom of Sky-World.

Sky-Woman fell and fell for what seemed like many hours. Then, just as she was about to hit the water, a group of water birds saw her and decided to save her by carrying her on their backs.

They lifted her up as high as they were able, but could not return her to Sky-World. Looking to the water below, the water birds saw a turtle swimming along the surface.

Shouting to the turtle they said, "Turtle, this woman is getting pretty heavy and we are tired. Can we place her on your back?"

The Turtle agreed and soon the birds gently placed Sky-Woman on the back of the turtle.

Thanking the water birds for saving her, Sky-Woman looked around and decided that the place was pretty empty and could use some decorating. So gathering all the animals around her, she asked them if they would help. She explained that as she fell from Sky-World, she was able to grab a piece of root from the Great Tree, and that if they could get some soil from the bottom of the great ocean she could plant it.

So deciding to help, the animals went down one by one to the bottom of the ocean. Each time they would go deeper and deeper, but would soon give up as it was too deep and they would run out of breath too soon. This went on and on until there was only one animal left who hadn't tried.

Stepping forward, Muskrat said, "I will give it a try."

So, Muskrat took three deep breaths, wiggled first one foot, then the other, scratched an unbearable itch, took three more deep breaths and jumped into the water with a splash. Soon he was out of sight as he dove deeper and deeper into the dark ocean.

Meanwhile, Sky-Woman and the other animals waited on Turtle's back. But Muskrat did not return. Eventually they gave up, and said, "Poor Muskrat, he must have drowned."

Just as these words left their lips, a limp, lifeless body that was once Muskrat floated to the surface. Sky-Woman carefully picked up the drowned animal and placed him beside her on the Turtle's back.

"Poor Muskrat, he must have swam so deep that he could not get back up in time for air."

Looking in his small fist she saw clenched within, a small bit of soil. Muskrat had made it to the bottom of the ocean, but had given his life to do this.

Carefully taking the bit of soil from Muskrat's fist, she placed it in the middle of the Great Turtle's back and sang a mournful song for Muskrat. Thanking him for his sacrifice, she began to walk around the little bit of soil in a counter-clockwise fashion. This being the direction of the sun.

As Sky-Woman walked around that bit of soil, it began to grow and grow. She continued to walk and walk, and as she walked, she chanted the songs that she knew from Sky-World. She continued to walk for many days and eventually she gave birth to a daughter who was fully grown.

Then Sky-Woman and that daughter began to walk and sing those songs, and go around that bit of soil some more.

Many days pasted and soon the daughter fainted from exhaustion, and when she awoke she had two arrows on her chest. Sky-Woman knew immediately that her daughter would bear twin sons. So helping her daughter stand, they continued to walk for many more days until they created an island on the back of that turtle.

Meanwhile, while those twin boys were in the younger woman, they argued as twins often do. The Right-Handed Twin wanted to be born in the usual way, but the Left-Handed Twin said "No", he wanted to come out their mother's arm-pit. And so when they were born, the Right-Handed Twin was born in the usual manner, while the Left-Handed Twin was born from their mother's arm-pit, thus killing their mother on the spot.

Seeing this, Sky-Woman buried her daughter by placing soil on top of her body, and soon from her daughter's grave grew corn, beans and squash. Then from her heart grew the most sacred of all medicine; tobacco. These are the four sacred medicines of the Mohawk people.

The grandmother, who was Sky-Woman, then raised the twins and soon discovered that the Right-Handed Twin and the Left-Handed Twin had the power of creation. The Right-Handed Twin made gentle hills, beautiful smelling flowers, helpful plants, quiet brooks to fish in, fireflies and other beautiful creatures. While his brother the Left-Handed Twin created snakes, animals of prey, thorn bushes, thunder and lightning and the other more disturbing attributes of today's world like taxes and global warming.

Together the Twins created man with his many attributes. The Right-Handed Twin believed in diplomacy as conflict resolution, while the Left-Handed Twin believed in conflict as a form of resolution. They were very different and very opposite each other, but what they created became an important part of Turtle Island and this realm.

After a time, their grandmother Sky-Woman died, as all things must die. Saddened by the loss of their grandmother, but overtaken by greed, the twins fought over her body and eventually tore it apart. Enraged by this, the Left-Handed Twin threw the head of their grandmother high into the sky, and there it remains for all time as Grandmother Moon.

It soon became clear to the twins that they could not live together. So both agreed to dwell in different realms of the world. and so the Right-Handed Twin lives in the daylight realm while the Left-Handed Twin became a dweller of the night. Each twin has their own special role that they must perform, and continue doing to this day.

And so that is why we call Sky-Woman, Grandmother Moon, and her daughter Mother Earth, the one who gave us our *Four Sacred Medicines*. We also call the Right-Handed Twin brother Sun, and the Left-Handed Twin brother Night.

Author's Notes: I have twin sons, Jesse and Dylan, so I guess that's why they are like night and day.

NDN KARS

Music and lyrics by Keith Secola

Verse 1.
I've been driving in my Indian Car
Hear the pound of the wheel drumming in my brain
My dash is dusty, my plates are expired
Please Mr. Officer, let me explain
I got to make it to a Pow Wow tonight
I'll be singing 49, down by the riverside
Looking for a sugar, riding in my Indian Car

Verse 2.
Got my T-bird in the glove box, I ain't got no spare
Got a feather from an eagle, I ain't got no care
The road is empty in my bottle of desire
Daylight is breaking, the sun touches fire
I got to make another Pow Wow tonight
I'll be singing 49, down by the riverside
Looking for a sugar, riding in my Indian Car

Verse 3.
My car is dented, the radiator steams
One headlight don't work, the radio can scream
I got a sticker says "Indian Power"
I stuck it on my bumper, that's what holds my car together
We're on a circuit of an Indian dream
We don't get old, we just get younger
When we're flying down the highway
Riding in our Indian Cars

Repeat
We're on a circuit of an Indian dream
We don't get old, we just get younger
When we're flying down the highway
Riding in our Indian Cars
Riding in our Indian Cars
Riding in our Indian Cars

NDN Stuff

I've been listening to Keith Secola's music for some time now, and find that it encompasses the spirit, humour and irony of being NDN. He is perhaps the most influential artist in the NDN music community today, with critics dubbing him "as the Native versions of both Neil Young and Bruce Springsteen"[1]. *NDN Kars* has become the "Contemporary Native American Anthem" and for this reason I felt it fitting as the father's travelling song. I would like to invite you to visit Keith Secola's website and read how he wrote *NDN Kars*. His website can be found at: http://www.secola.com/blog/ndn_kars/

Pow Wows

The Pow Wow is a social gathering in which hundreds of NDN people get together to celebrate the renewal of life and to meet old friends and family. In the past the Pow Wow had religious significance, and for some Nations it is still a time to offer prays to the Great Spirit or Creator. (For this reason it is asked that visitors respect the opening and closing ceremonies in which hats and pictures are not allowed.)

The Pow Wow is a major part of many NDN lives, and during the weekend you can count on at least one Pow Wow happening between the months of June and September. Many families will go on 'the circuit', travelling North America to attend a different Pow Wow each weekend. In most cases each Pow Wow will be hosted by a particular Nation across Turtle Island, and so this will give ample opportunity to experience many different NDN cultures.

I once spoke with an Elder on the way back from a Pow Wow on Christian Island (Ontario), he told me that he used to do 'the circuit' as a drummer, and that there were more Pow Wows on Turtle Island than you could possibly attend in one summer. But he then added, "... it was a lot of fun trying." I always welcome the chance to *listen* to Elders and while it's not always possible, a Pow Wow is a great place to do this.

At the Pow Wow you'll find good NDN food (frybread and corn soup being my favourites), NDN crafts and of course, competition dancing and drumming. These two activities go hand in hand, and you won't find one without the other.

Drums and Drumming

For a person attending a Pow Wow for the first time, the most memorable aspect (other than having so many NDNs gathered in one place) is the sound and the ***feel*** of the drum. The *thump, thump, thump* of the drum is probably the most pervasive aspect of any Pow Wow. Typically located within the center of the grounds, dancers can be found dancing around the drum in a counter-clockwise or clockwise rotation depending on the Nation. Typically Mohawks would dance in a counter-clockwise rotation (according to our creation story), but will dance according to the traditions of the Nation we are visiting.

"The drum is more than a musical instrument to those who own and play it. It has a life of its own. Some drum groups have ceremonies to have their drums blessed and named. The drum is regarded as having its own powerful spirit. Gifts are made to it and some have their own sacred medicine pipes. In some traditions the drum symbolizes the heartbeat; in others, the powerful medicine of thunder. The term "drum" also refers to the drum group itself." [2]

'Singing 49'

A *49* song is one in which several lines are sung in the NDN language and then a final line is sung in English. There may be a larger definition of the *49*'s but they seem to be regarded in most cases as social songs that are entertaining and often risqué. Keith Secola plays what is considered *electric 49*.

[1] http://aboriginalpeopleschoice.com/artists/keith-secola/
[2] http://www.snowwowl.com/pwmeaning.html#drum

BIBLIOGRAPHY

http://en.wikipedia.org/wiki/Iroquoian_languages
http://www.fourdirectionsteachings.com/transcripts/mohawk.html
http://www.haudenosauneeconfederacy.com

ONLINE RESOURCES

http://www.haudenosauneeconfederacy.com/index.html
http://www.mohawknation.org
http://www.kahnawake.com
http://www.bigorrin.org/mohawk_kids.htm
http://www.mbq-tmt.org
http://wahtamohawks.ca
http://www.akwesasne.ca
http://www.thecanadianencyclopedia.ca/en/article/mohawk/
http://www.native-languages.org/iroquois.htm

SUGGESTED READING

Mohawk Interruptus: Political Life Across the Borders of Settler States, Audra Simpson, Duke University Press Books (May 9, 2014)

Wasáse: Indigenous Pathways of Action and Freedom, Taiaiake Alfred, University of Toronto Press, Higher Education Division; First Edition edition (August 1, 2005)

Heeding the Voices of Our Ancestors: Kahnawake Mohawk Politics and the Rise of Native Nationalism, Gerald Robert Alfred, Oxford University Press (September 21, 1995)

POW WOW INFORMATION

http://www.akwesasnepowwow.com
http://www.kahnawakepowwow.com
http://www.powwows.com

ABOUT THE AUTHOR

Deron *Sasonake* Douglas is a Kanien'kehá:ka (Mohawk) artist with roots in the Kahnawà:ke Mohawk Territory. Originally working with oil on canvas (although he has dabbled in stone and wood carving, clay, photography, water color, acrylic and print-making), he started illustrating book covers in 2000 and has created more than 1000 cover images for various publications. He recently returned to his favourite medium and continues to sign his oil paintings with his Kanien'kehá name as he did more than 35 years ago.

Sasonake grew up within a culture of oral storytelling, and remembers the many stories told by his father and grandmother around the kitchen table. His favourite, which is one told by his father, is called *Lahk'ahni:'s Farm* and is a true ghost story which has haunted his family for many generations. He hopes to publish this illustrated story sometime in the near future.

He continues to visit elementary classrooms to share his traditional and non-traditional stories, and to promote First Nation culture whenever the opportunity presents itself.

While he would state that he is a 'Jack–of–all–Trades, and Master–of–None', he does have formal training in the fine arts (art history and photography), design, computer science, social science and education.

CPSIA information can be obtained
at www.ICGtesting.com
Printed in the USA
LVIC04n2226270215
428704LV00003B/4
* 9 7 8 1 7 7 1 1 5 2 1 8 1 *